Howard The Horrible Gets Even

Gary Richmond

WORD
Kids!

Dallas • London • Sydney • Singapore

VIEW FROM THE ZOO STORIES are based on the real-life adventures of Gary Richmond, a veteran of the Los Angeles Zoo, minister, counselor, and camp nature speaker. Gary has three children and lives in Chino Hills, California, with his wife, Carol.

Library of Congress Cataloging-in-Publication Data

Richmond, Gary, 1944-
    Howard the horrible gets even / by Gary Richmond ;
        illustrated by Bruce Day.
        p. cm. — (A View from the zoo series)
    Summary: A Christian zookeeper relates an anecdote
about an ill-tempered ostrich and draws a parallel with
God's lesson about being kind to those who are mean.
    ISBN 0-8499-0744-6 : $7.99
    1. Kindness — Religious aspects — Christianity —
Juvenile literature. [1. Christian life. 2. Ostriches. 3.
Zoos.] I. Day, Bruce, ill. II. Title. III. Series: Richmond,
Gary, 1944- View from the zoo series.
BV4647.K5R52 1990
242'.62 — dc20   90-12334
                                                        CIP
                                                         AC

This book is dedicated to Summer, Roman, Scarlet, Jubal and Amber Day, whose father, Bruce, is a very fine illustrator.

Hi, I'm Gary Richmond, and I'm a zoo keeper. As a zoo keeper, I've learned a lot about God's wonderful animals. At the same time, I've learned a lot about God.

This true story is about a mean, dangerous ostrich I called Howard the Horrible.

Now, zoo keepers love animals, right? Well, that's true most of the time. But it's not true all of the time.

I am an animal lover. After working at the zoo for seven years, I can say this: I loved all of the animals some of the time. I loved some of the animals all of the time. But I didn't love all of the animals all of the time.

Perhaps you're an animal lover. You might think you can love all animals all the time. If so, I know you've never met Howard the ostrich! If you had met Howard, you would know this: some animals are like some people. They can be rude, ugly, gross, mean and horrible.

The ostrich is a huge bird with beautiful eyes. Why, you could hang your coat on their long, gorgeous eyelashes. But when you look deep into their eyes, you'll find that nobody is home. Ostriches seem to have no brains!

Even the Bible says that ostriches are not too smart: "she steps on her eggs and breaks them." It does say, however, that she runs like the wind. Somehow, though, running fast does not excuse her carelessness.

Birds should fly, don't you think? Now God made over 10,000 different kinds of birds. And only four kinds of birds don't fly: the kiwi, the emu, the cassowary and, you guessed it, the ostrich. I think God knew they weren't too smart. So, He decided the world would be safer if these birds stayed on the ground.

Howard was moved to my section of the zoo. He was too dangerous to his keeper in the main zoo. The keeper couldn't do his work because he was too busy fighting off Howard. You see, Howard weighed over 200 pounds. He could kill a man if he wanted to. In fact, Howard spent a lot of energy trying to hurt George Gast, his keeper.

I wasn't really excited about being Howard's new
keeper either. But caring for the extra zoo animals was my
job. I would take care of Howard until he was sold to
another zoo. My senior keeper, Al Franklin, decided to help
me. He would stand guard whenever I was cleaning and
feeding in Howard's yard. I was glad to have Al there.

When we went into Howard's area, he would begin his mating dance. He would crouch down and fan his wings out one at a time. Then he would rock back and forth. He acted as if Al and I were lady ostriches. We were not impressed, though. This made Howard very angry. That's when he would attack us.

Most people don't know that ostriches are very dangerous. They have powerful legs with huge, three-inch toenails that can dig into a person's body.

Al controlled Howard with a leaf rake. He put it under Howard's chin and made him back up. That way, Al could keep Howard safely away from me while I cleaned the yard. It worked well. Several days went by without any problems. The bad days came when Al went on vacation. Being a bit proud, I didn't want to ask for help. George Gast had never asked for help when he kept Howard. So, I wouldn't get help either. Besides, I had a plan: take charge, I thought. Show Howard who's boss.

The first day Al was gone, I went into Howard's yard alone. I ran at Howard with the rake as if I were attacking him. It surprised him, and he ran from me. The yard was huge. I ran him all the way to the back of it. He paced back and forth nervously because there was nowhere else to run.

"Listen to me, Howard," I said firmly. "We will do fine if you stay away from me." Then I was free to clean and feed the deer and pigmy goats. They shared the yard with Howard. But I kept my eye on him all the time, just in case.

I wondered why George had such a terrible problem with Howard. I thought he should have just been more forceful. For a week Howard kept his distance from me. If he didn't, he got a pointed rake reminder. That kept him in line.

Finally, Howard decided he had had enough of me. I don't know what made him change. But one day when I came to the yard, there was Howard. He was waiting at the gate, so close that it was hard to open. He was looking at me as if I were his girlfriend again.

I pushed my way in. Then I put the rake under his chin and yelled, "Get back, Howard! We're not going to start this again."

Howard pushed his neck against the rake. Then he surprised me by leaping and kicking. The rake kept him a safe distance away. Soon Howard began to back up. I was feeling pretty much in control. So, I backed him to the edge of the yard.

For good measure, I jabbed the rake toward Howard to threaten him. When I did, the end of the rake fell off. Howard and I both stared at it in surprise. Then we both decided the same thing: I was in real trouble!

Our eyes met for a moment. There was angry fire in Howard's eyes and fear in mine. Howard the Horrible's eyes narrowed. He was no longer a goofy-looking, flightless bird. He was a dragon. And I was a knight — a swordless knight without any armor. This dragon didn't know much. But he knew an unarmed knight when he saw one. Howard was not afraid anymore.

Suddenly, Howard leaped high in the air toward me. He was kicking hard with his giant toenails. He barely missed me! When he landed I could feel the ground shake. My heart was beating like a rapid-fire machine gun. I turned and ran as fast as I could. I made about ten yards while he was recovering from his leap. Then he began to chase me.

An ostrich can run as fast as a race horse; so, Howard began catching up quickly. Fifty yards away, in the middle of the yard, was a large metal hay feeder. The feeder was about thirty feet from the gate. I had to make it to the hay feeder. If not, Howard would surely kick me to death. I knew it, and he knew it.

I ran with all my might, straining every muscle in my legs. I leaned forward to get as much speed as possible. I made it to the hay feeder! I grabbed it and made a quick turn. Howard was on one side and I was on the other. I was trembling, and my legs were wobbly and weak.

Our eyes met again, and Howard stared at me. He had the look of a hunter. I was his prey. He began to stalk me slowly around and around the hay feeder. My heart was pounding harder than ever. I knew we couldn't keep this up forever. So, I began to stare at the gate. Could I run thirty feet, pull up the latch and shut the gate before Howard the Horrible squashed me like a grape? Meanwhile, we kept circling the hay feeder.

Finally, Howard stopped and pretended to give up the chase. He looked away. But I knew he was only trying to trap me. I faked a run to the gate. Howard was out of the chute like a rocket after me!

"Fooled you, Howard!" I said. "You'll have to do better than that to catch me."

We circled the feeder again. Then Howard saw some grain on the ground that he pecked at. I wasn't sure, but I thought he forgot about me. Howard was on one side of the feeder. I was on the other side by the gate. I decided that now was the time to make a run for it.

I pushed off the feeder. I knew I had better be right. I had run about ten feet before Howard turned. When he did, he was quick.

I grabbed the gate and looked back. Howard the
Horrible was chasing me at full speed. His eyes looked like
raging fires. I yanked up the latch and backed up slightly to
get the gate open. I jumped around the gate just as Howard
ran into it, knocking it shut. For good measure, he jumped
and kicked the fence. It shook under the force of his blow.

Howard stomped around nervously for several minutes. He was daring me to come back into the yard. I knew I couldn't let Howard get away with this. No one would be safe in this yard again. So, I found another zoo keeper and explained the problem. I asked him if he would clean the yard while I took control of Howard again. He knew how mean Howard was, so he was glad to help.

We both took shovels and rakes. I pulled hard on the end of my rake. I wanted to be sure it would not fall off this time. We stepped into the yard. Howard was on us like a tick on a hound. But I was ready for him. I put the rake under his chin and pushed. I kept a safe distance. In a few minutes I had Howard moving wherever I wanted him to go. I didn't hurt him; I just showed him who was boss. That way we could safely care for Howard and his yard mates.

I never went into Howard's yard alone again. All I had to do was ask for help until Al returned. Everyone was glad to say yes. They knew they might need this kind of help sometime, too.

When I think about it today, life has always been a little like a zoo. Some people remind me of Howard the Horrible. Don't you know some people who are not very nice to be around?

Well, guess what? God teaches us to be kind even to people who are mean. You see, I could have been mean to Howard. Or I could have hurt him for chasing me. But then I would have been just as bad as Howard. The best thing for me to do was this: let Howard know I would not go along with his mean tricks. But I would still be his friend and take care of him.

The next time you meet someone like Howard the Horrible, be nice to them. But don't go along with the bad things they do. After all, that's what Jesus did. When his enemies hurt him, he just loved them back. He even offered to save them. Don't you want to be like Jesus?